THE MAHABHARATA
CHILDREN'S ILLUSTRATED CLASSICS

THE WAR *is* DECLARED

Retold by **CHARU AGARWAL DHANDIA**
Art **KAVITA SINGH KALE** *Design* **RACHITA RAKYAN**

Published by
Rupa Publications India Pvt. Ltd 2020
7/16, Ansari Road, Daryaganj
New Delhi 110002

Sales centres:
Allahabad Bengaluru Chennai
Hyderabad Jaipur Kathmandu
Kolkata Mumbai

Edition copyright © Rupa Publications Pvt. Ltd 2020

All rights reserved.
No part of this publication may be reproduced, transmitted,
or stored in a retrieval system, in any form or by any means, electronic, mechanical, photocopying,
recording or otherwise,
without the prior permission of the publisher.

ISBN: 978-81-291-4977-0

First impression 2020

10 9 8 7 6 5 4 3 2 1

The moral right of the author has been asserted.

Printed at Nutech Print Services - India

This book is sold subject to the condition that it shall not, by way of trade or otherwise, be lent, resold, hired out, or otherwise circulated, without the publisher's prior consent, in any form of binding or cover other than that in which it is published.

Charu Agarwal Dhandia weaves together her two biggest passions—studying Indian classical literature and creative storytelling. She is an economist by training and works in the social development space.

Kavita Singh Kale's background as an artist and a designer enables her to draw a thin line between design following functionality and pure self-expression. This has helped her evolve as a transmedia artist. Her work includes art installations, children's books, comics, paintings and videos.

Rachita Rakyan combines over 15 years of expertise in graphic design and art direction with deep understanding of functionality and aesthetics across print, publishing, branding and digital media.

CONTENTS

KURU DYNASTY	*IV–V*
KEY CHARACTERS	*VI–VII*
PANDAVAS DECLARE WAR	1
KRISHNA IN DWARKA	13
SANJAYA'S BOON	19
KARNA AND KUNTI	25
ARMIES ARE FORMED	31
ARJUNA AND KRISHNA	39

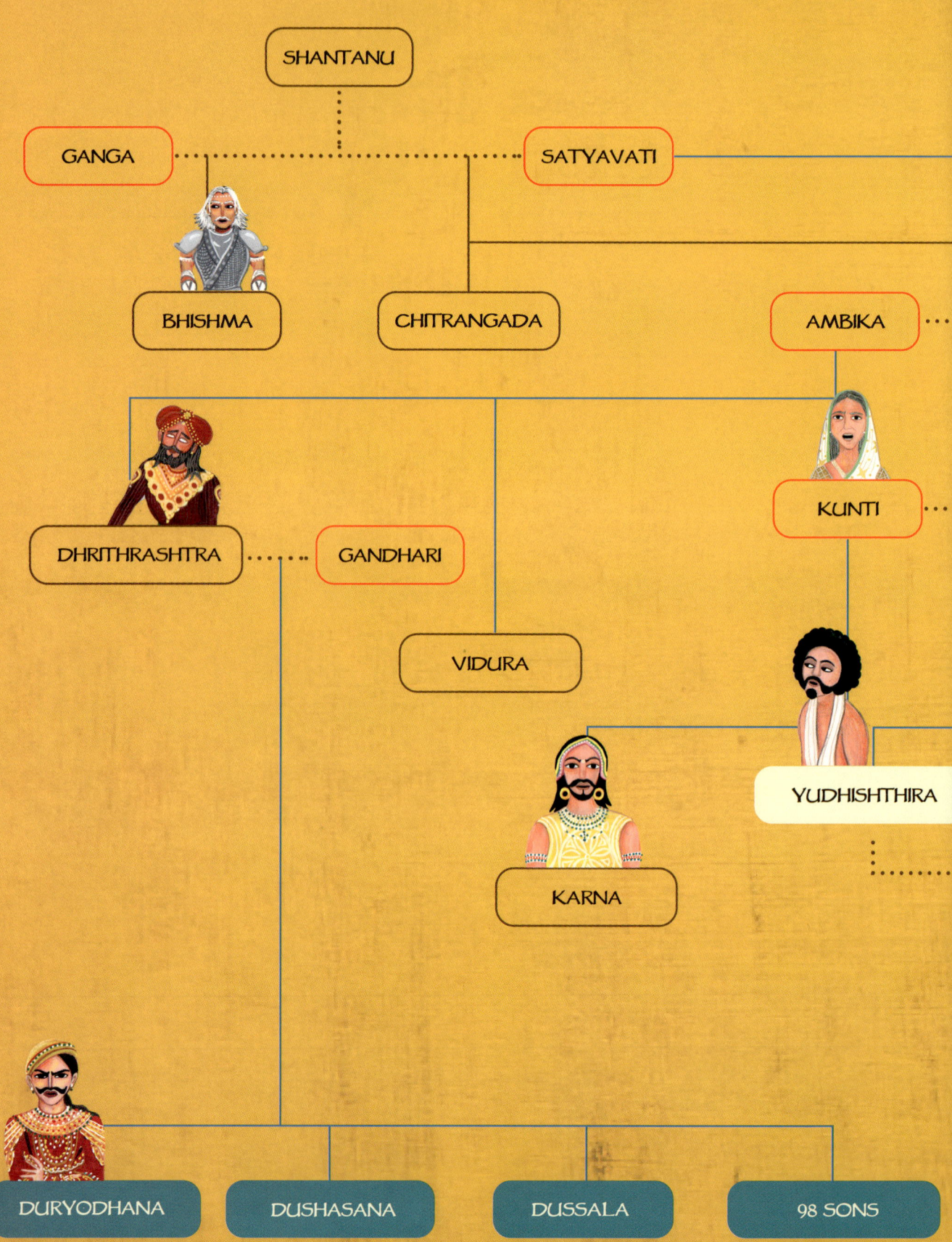

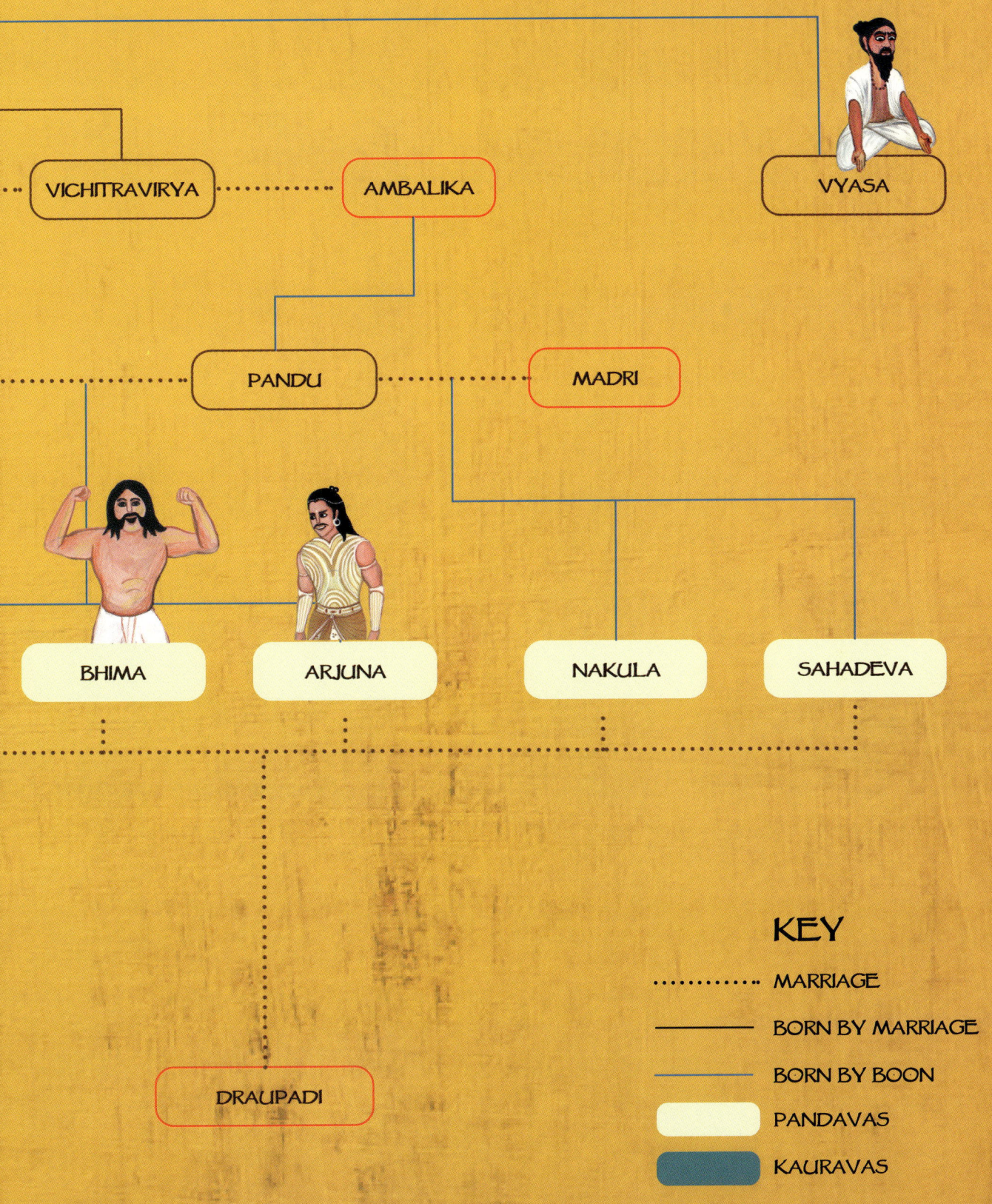

KEY CHARACTERS

DURYODHANA

Duryodhana was the eldest brother amongst the Kauravas and born to princess Gandhari as a blessing from sage Vyasa. He was very jealous of the Pandavas.

YUDHISHTHIRA

Yudhishthira was the eldest Pandava born to Kunti as a blessing from Lord Dharma. He ruled Indraprastha and later Hastinapur. Yudhishthira proved to be a great ruler and was known for his virtues of honesty, loyalty, justice, tolerance and brotherhood.

ARJUNA

Arjuna was the third of the Pandava brothers born to Kunti by the boon of Lord Indra. He was the greatest archer in the country. Arjuna was Dronacharya's favourite pupil.

KRISHNA

Krishna was the prince of Dwarka and cousin brother of the Pandavas and Kauravas. He was a great friend and advisor to Arjuna and loved the Pandavas dearly. He played a critical role in the creation of Indraprastha and later in the Kurukshetra War.

KARNA

Karna was born to young Kunti by the boon of Lord Surya. He was raised by a charioteer Adhiratha and his wife Radha. Later, he became, a supremely skilled archer known for his loyalty and friendship with Duryodhana.

BHISHMA

Born as Devavrata to King Shantanu and Goddess Ganga, he came to be known as Bhishma, meaning the firm. He was an unparalleled archer and the greatest warrior of that time.

PANDAVAS DECLARE WAR

Duryodhana, the eldest of the Kauravas, had cheated his cousins, the Pandavas, in a game of dice. The Pandavas had lost their kingdom and everything else that belonged to them. They had to live in exile. They dressed like brahmins and lived in a small hut in the forest.

One day, their mighty cousins—Krishna and Balarama came to meet them in the forest. The princes were very happy to see them and welcomed them warmly.

When Balarama saw how the Pandavas were living in exile, he was upset. He said angrily, 'You have spent thirteen years in this forest because of the evil Duryodhana. He and his uncle Shakuni cheated you in the game. No one stopped them! Now the Kauravas must return your kingdom Indraprastha to you.'

'But would Duryodhana return Indraprastha?' the Pandavas wondered.
'If they refuse to do so, we will declare war against the Kauravas!'

Yudhishthira replied, 'But the Kauravas are our brothers. We do not want to fight with them. If they refuse to return Indraprastha, it is okay. We will ask for five villages only. We shall be happy with that.'
'O Krishna, you have always helped us. Would you talk to Duryodhana on our behalf?' requested Yudhishthira.

Krishna agreed and left for Hastinapur.

Krishna entered King Dhrithrashtra's court and said, 'O King, the Pandavas have spent thirteen years in the forest. It is now time for them to return. You should give their kingdom back to them. Let there be peace!'

But Duryodhana was full of pride and greed. He came forward angrily. 'I will not give anything to the Pandavas! The kingdom is mine! They will have to fight with me to get it back!' he shouted.

This made Krishna furious. He said, 'Duryodhana, the Pandavas want only what is theirs. They are not asking for anything more. But once again, you are being unfair to them.'

Krishna looked around and announced, 'Now there will be war in Kurukshetra! The brave Pandavas will destroy you!' Everyone present was shocked. Some people requested Duryodhana to change his decision. But he did not listen.

Krishna left the palace angrily.

KRISHNA IN DWARKA

The news of war spread all across the country. The Pandavas and Kauravas began forming their armies for a mighty battle. The Pandavas and Kauravas both wanted Krishna's help in the war. So Duryodhana and Arjuna reached Dwarka to meet Krishna.

Duryodhana saw Krishna sleeping in his chambers. He sat on a chair near his bed and waited for him to wake up. Soon Arjuna also entered. He sat quietly near Krishna's feet and waited. In some time, Krishna woke up. He was surprised to see both Duryodhana and Arjuna.

Duryodhana said, 'O Krishna! The Kauravas need your help in the war with the Pandavas!'
'Dear Krishna, we Pandavas cannot do without you!' said Arjuna.

Krishna looked at the two brothers. He said, 'Both of you are my cousins. I should not favour any one of you. So I give you two choices. Either, I will be your charioteer in the war or I will give you my entire army.'

At once, Arjuna said, 'I want you to be with me, dear Krishna! It is enough if you are beside us.'
Duryodhana was filled with joy. He said, 'I want your army.'
Krishna agreed.

SANJAYA'S BOON

K ing Dhrithrashtra trusted his charioteer Sanjaya and loved him dearly.

One day, he called Sanjaya and said sadly, 'I am blind and will not be able to see the war! I do not know what to do.'

At that moment, the great sage Vyasa appeared and said,

'O King, I can give you a boon to help you see the war. But will your heart not break to see the princes fight with each other?'

King Dhrithrashtra replied, 'You are right. They are all my children. I will not be able to see brothers fighting each other.
O sage, tell me what to do!'

Vyasa thought for a moment and said, 'I will give Sanjaya the boon of vision. He will be able to see the battle from wherever he is. It will be as if he is present in the battlefield.

Sanjaya will describe the battle to you. In this way, you will know everything that happens.'
So sage Vyasa blessed Sanjaya.

KARNA AND KUNTI

Kunti was heartbroken to hear that there would be a war between the Pandavas and Kauravas. They were all her sons! She decided to meet Karna secretly.

Kunti said, 'Karna, I have a secret to tell you.'

Kunti began narrating a story to Karna, while he listened intently.

'Long ago, I had used a magic chant out of curiosity and you were born to me. I was very young and did not know what to do. I put you in a basket and floated it in the river.

A charioteer called Adhiratha found you and raised you like his son.'

'The Pandavas are your brothers. Do not go to war with them. I do not want to lose any of you!'

Karna replied, 'Mother, Duryodhana helped me and made me a King when others called me Sutaputra. He has always been good to me. Arjuna is Duryodhana's enemy. So he is my enemy also. Forgive me Mother, I am bound by my loyalty to Duryodhana.'

Kunti realized Karna was doing the right thing. She blessed Karna and returned in grief.

ARMIES ARE FORMED

Dhrishtadyumna was Draupadi's brother. He was brave and fearless. Yudhishthira decided to make him the chief of the Pandava army.

In the Kaurava camp, Duryodhana asked the brave Bhishma to become the chief of the army. Bhishma did not know what to do. He loved the Pandavas and Kauravas equally. How could he take sides? He was their grandfather!

Bhishma thought for a while and said, 'Duryodhana, before I agree to lead your army, I have two conditions. First, I will not attack the Pandava brothers in the war.'
Duryodhana agreed.
'Second, Karna will not enter the battleground as long as I am leading the army.'

In his heart, Bhishma knew that Karna was a great warrior. Only Karna could defeat Arjuna in battle. He did not want that to happen. This is why Bhishma made the second condition.

Karna heard Bhishma's condition and said angrily, 'I promise not to enter the battleground as long as Bhishma is the chief of the Kaurava army.'

ARJUNA AND KRISHNA

Soon it was the day of the battle. The sun shone brightly. The Pandava and Kaurava armies stood facing each other. Red and blue flags fluttered on both sides of the Kurukshetra battlefield.

Thousands of horses, elephants and warriors marched forward. Loud trumpets and conches blew to signal that the army was ready.

Even though they were now enemies, Yudhishthira went to the other side of the battleground where the Kauravas were lined up. He bowed in respect before his grandfather Bhishma, guru Dronacharya and his uncles and cousin brothers.

Deeply touched by his gesture of courtesy and humility, they blessed Yudhishthira and the other Pandavas.

Arjuna sat in his chariot with Krishna as his charioteer. But seeing his cousins, guru and Pitamah Bhishma on the enemy side, Arjuna became very sad.

'I grew up with them. They are my family! How can I attack them now?' he thought.

Arjuna said, 'Look, there stands the great Bhishma, my grandfather. There is my guru Dronacharya. I have loved and respected them all my life. Those are my cousins, Duryodhana and Dushasana. O Krishna, I do not have the heart to raise my arrows at them!'

Arjuna threw down his weapons.

Then Krishna spoke. 'Prince Arjuna,' he said calmly. 'You are born in the world with a purpose. Duryodhana and his brothers have evil intentions. Your purpose is to help the people of your country get rid of this evil. For this, you will have to be brave, fight the Kaurava army and win this war!'

But Arjuna could not agree.

Now Krishna said firmly, 'Once you enter the battlefield, you have no family or friend. Your effort should be to kill evil people such as Duryodhana, Dushasana and Shakuni. It will make the world a better and more peaceful place to live in. You have to give your best to fulfil your duty and purpose.

Now Arjuna, pick up your weapons and fight! Do not think anymore! This is the most important duty you have.
Go ahead and fulfil it!'

Arjuna was convinced now. He picked up his bow and arrow, and got ready for battle. Krishna blew his conch signalling for the great war to begin.
And the great war of Kurukshetra began!

TITLES IN THIS SERIES

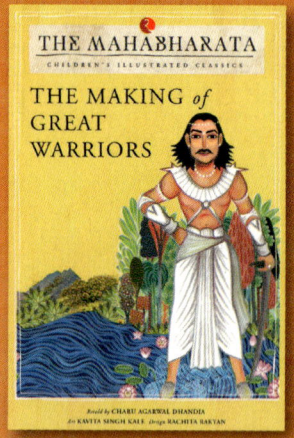
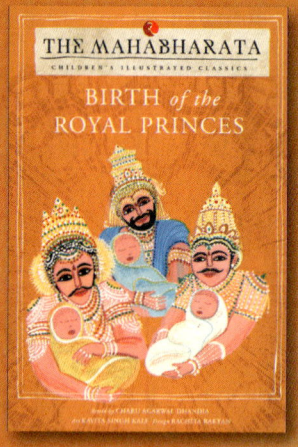
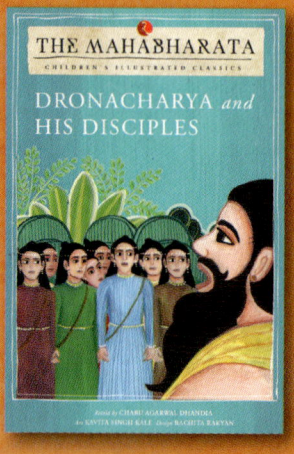
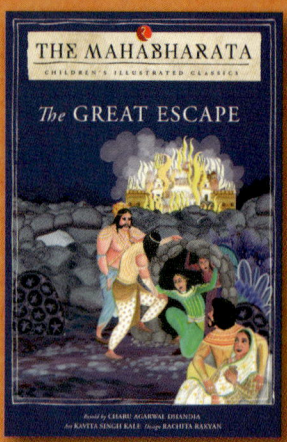
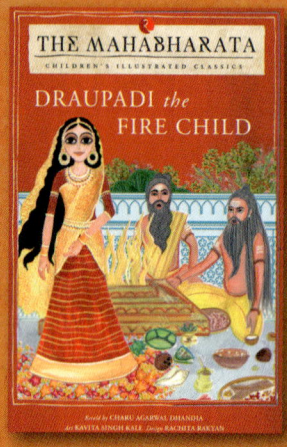
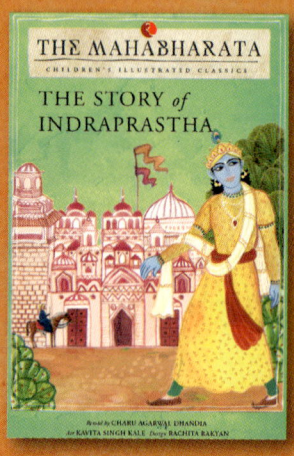
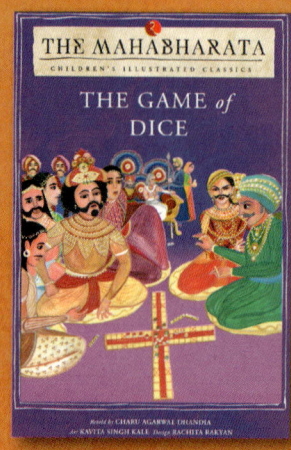
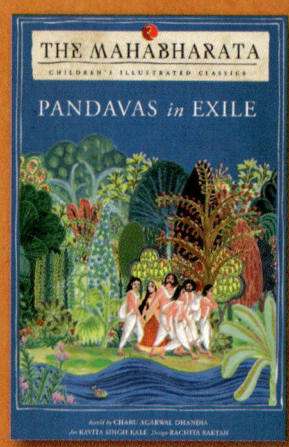
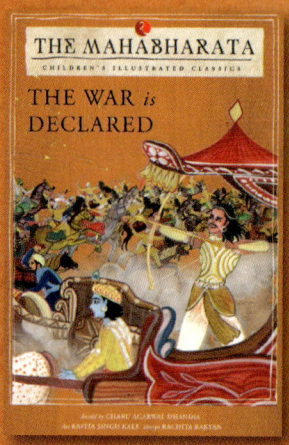
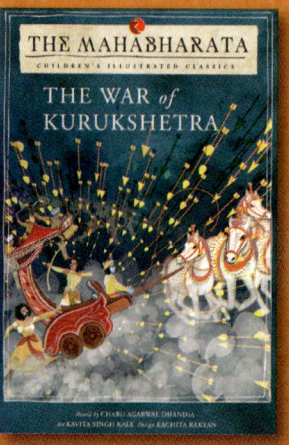